✳ Stardom! ✳

✳ Fame and fortune ✳ could be one step away!

✳ Welcome to ✳

Fame School

For another fix of

read

Fame School

Battle of the Bands

Cindy Jefferies

For Adrienne, Luke,
and of course Cat.

First published in 2007 by Usborne Publishing Ltd., Usborne House,
83-85 Saffron Hill, London EC1N 8RT, England. www.usborne.com

A CIP catalogue record for this book is available from the British Library.

JFMAMJJ SOND/07

ISBN 9780746078839

Printed in Great Britain.

1 And the Winners Are...

"I can't *bear* it, Lolly!" groaned Chloe, clutching onto her best friend's arm. "If they make us wait any longer I'll *die!*"

Chloe was waiting backstage at a large theatre in London, with competitors from all around the country, while the judges deliberated over their performances in the National Battle of the Bands competition.

"Me too," agreed Lolly, looking anxious. "*Surely* we'll have the results soon?"

It was a huge moment. Everyone backstage had just taken part in a new competition to find the very best school bands. That was exciting enough, but it would be just the beginning for the winners. The four successful bands, two junior and two senior, would be going to Italy, to represent their country in an International Battle of the Bands competition.

Chloe and her friends were pupils at Rockley Park, the well-known school for students who want to make it in the music business, and the dedicated staff had spent ages deciding who should represent the school.

One group of vocalists and one band had been chosen to represent each age range. Chloe was the best junior singer in the school, but her voice was unusual, it didn't blend in well with a variety of other voices. So she was thrilled and relieved when the teachers chose her to sing with a rock band, especially as she was such good friends with Danny, the drummer.

Last year Chloe had hated her teacher's suggestion that she should try singing with a band. But that had led to an exciting appearance on a TV show. Now she loved being a lead singer, and sang with Danny's band as often as she could.

"Ssh. Listen!" said Danny to the girls. "I think they're ready."

All the Rockley Park students gathered together as the big, backstage screen showed the judges going back onstage. It was totally quiet now. Everyone was watching the screen, clutching good-luck tokens, crossing their fingers or just waiting, and hoping for the best.

"First, the senior winners," said the chairman of the judges.

The six girl vocalists of the Rockley Park seniors held hands and closed their eyes. Chloe crossed her fingers for them, but they were all bitterly disappointed as the chairman announced that the winning vocalists were from a rival school. The senior rock band didn't fare any better either, though the judges did say that it had been hard to choose between them and the winners.

"So they were only just beaten into second place," said Lolly.

"But second isn't good enough," said Chloe sadly. She looked at the dejected seniors, who were all trying to put on brave faces. They had congratulated the winners, but it was obvious the only thing they wanted now was to leave the glitzy occasion, and go home. Chloe gulped. The junior results came next. Was Rockley Park going to come away with absolutely nothing?

"If anything, the juniors were harder to judge than the seniors," said the chairman. "But in the end we decided that Pink Toffee, the all-girl vocalists from Sedge Combe School were the winners."

"Well done," Lolly said bravely to the winning girls. Then she turned away to hug her twin sister Pop, who was crying. Pop and Lolly, along with the three other singers in their group, The Rockley Five, had missed out on winning, like the seniors. But Chloe couldn't comfort them yet. She and the rest of her band were still waiting for their category to be announced.

"Don't worry," muttered Danny in her ear. "It's obvious that these judges just don't like the Rockley Park style. Judge Jim told me that this sort of thing happens." Judge Jim was the Head of Rock, and one of Chloe's favourite teachers. "It doesn't mean our bands are any worse than the others," Danny added.

Chloe wanted to hug Danny for being so positive, but there was no time.

"Last, but by no means least, the junior bands."

Chloe held her breath.

"There was a wide variety of bands in this group," the chairman said. "Most had opted to include at least one unusual instrument in their line-up, but in the end we chose a more traditional rock band of drums, bass and two guitars, with a lead singer."

Chloe closed her eyes. That was the Rockley Park line-up, but there were two other bands like that as well. She glanced at her band's guitarists. Ed and Ben had their arms round each other's shoulders. Tara, who had written the song and was the bassist, stood with her arms folded, trying to look her usual impassive self.

"The winning band," said the chairman, "after much deliberation, is Wizard Monkey Breath Scares the Horses from Rockley Park School!"

"Danny! We've done it! Tara! We're through!"

It was impossible to stand still. Chloe was jumping

up and down, her face filled with joy. "We're going to Italy!" she screamed at Tara through the cheers. "I've never been abroad before!"

Tara laughed. Even *she* looked excited now. They all linked arms, laughing and joking at how nerve-racking the announcement had been.

"Tara, you're *brilliant* at songwriting," said Chloe enthusiastically. "We would never have won without your composition. 'Sky Blue' is *such* a cool song."

"Come on, you two!" said Danny, grabbing Chloe's sleeve. "We've got to go back on and perform it again now."

He was right. Together with the rest of the band, Chloe ran onstage in her specially designed, sky-blue dress. There was a tumult of cheers from the enthusiastic audience. As she picked up her microphone, and waited for Danny to count them in, Chloe realized it really was true. They had won! They were going to represent their country. What an honour. And in ten days' time she would be in Italy!

2 A Frantic Week

After a long journey back to Rockley Park, and a very late night, Chloe and her roommates, Pop, Lolly and Tara, fell into bed absolutely exhausted. Even with all the excitement Chloe fell asleep very quickly and, when she woke in the morning, she had trouble remembering at first how much had happened.

She lay in bed with the sun streaming through the window and began to recall the most exciting day in her life so far. There had been the journey into London, the soundcheck, and then the performances. Everyone from Rockley Park had been so optimistic. After all, the school had a fantastic reputation for producing top-quality artists. And yet, only Chloe's band had managed to win.

She looked over at the twins' beds. Neither Pop nor Lolly was stirring yet, and when they did they wouldn't be bubbling over with excitement like Chloe was. Chloe felt sorry about that, but she couldn't help her own feelings fizzing up. She wanted to squeal with enthusiasm at her own good fortune, but held back. She looked the other way, at where Tara was still asleep in bed. She couldn't imagine how Tara could write such wonderful songs. When Chloe tried to do it the tune sounded awful and the lyrics were always terrible! But "Sky Blue" was a triumph.

Chloe wanted to talk to Tara about going to Italy but she didn't want to wake her up – Tara could be a bit prickly at the best of times – so instead she lay quietly for a bit longer.

What will it be like in Italy? she thought. *Will they speak any English? If not I'll never understand what I'm supposed to do!* But it would be the same for everyone. Dozens of different countries would be competing and there would probably be loads of students who didn't understand much Italian.

"Are you awake, Chloe?"

It was Lolly. Chloe sat up in bed and looked over at her friend. "Are you okay?" she asked.

"Of course I am." Lolly slid out of bed, tiptoed over to Chloe and sat on the side of her bed. "You must be *so* excited." She gave Chloe a big hug, squeezing all the breath out of her lungs.

Chloe nodded. "Yes I am. Of course I am!" she whispered. "But I don't want to be *too* excited. It's not fair on you and Pop and the others."

"Don't be silly!" Lolly's voice rose and she clapped her hand over her mouth with a giggle. "You know me," she went on more quietly. "Music isn't the only thing in my life. And Pop and I have travelled all over the world modelling, while you haven't ever been abroad before. It's *brilliant* that you won. The whole school is going to be so proud of you and the band."

"Do you think so?" said Chloe, grinning.

"Of *course*!" said Lolly. "And stop trying to be so modest. You know you deserved to win."

Pop sat up in her bed and looked blearily across the room. "I can't believe it's morning already," she muttered, stumbling out of bed and heading for the bathroom. A few minutes later she was back, fully awake and raring to go.

"Come on, Chloe, Tara. Get up!" she ordered in a loud voice. "I'm in the mood for a celebration. We did it! Rockley Park has a band going to the final of the International Battle of the Bands. How cool is that!"

Tara sat up groggily and put on her long-suffering face. "Imagine what she'd be like if The Rockley Five had got through," she grumbled to no one in particular.

Chloe giggled. Tara was right. Pop would have been unstoppable if she'd won! But Chloe was just grateful that Pop had got over her disappointment that The Rockley Five hadn't made it.

It didn't take long to get dressed and ready for breakfast. The four friends hurried over to the main building, and headed to the dining room. Danny, Ed and Ben were already there, and when everyone noticed Chloe and Tara, a big cheer went up from all the students. The news of their win had obviously travelled fast!

Straight after breakfast there was a special assembly, and Mrs. Sharkey, the Principal, asked the band up onstage to play their winning song. Everyone clapped and cheered again. Then, instead of going to lessons, Chloe and the band were asked to go straight to the Rock Department to see Judge Jim.

"Congratulations!" said the elderly teacher, his grey dreadlocks framing his beaming face. "I'm proud of *all* the Rockley bands, but I think you had somethin' extra special, an' I'm glad the judges saw it too. Now, we got lots of work to do before we fly out to Italy for the final."

"Are you coming to Italy with us?" asked Tara.

Judge Jim nodded. "And Mr. and Mrs. Player too," he told her. "We don' want you gettin' stressed out. We'll be there to help."

"Thank goodness for that," said Tara with feeling.

Chloe agreed. Judge Jim was her favourite teacher. He was the perfect person to have on an important occasion because he never got into a flap.

"I could do with going through the last verse a few times," said Ben. "I'm still not getting that riff quite right, no matter what I do."

"I need to speak to Mr. Player about my breathing," said Chloe.

"And I'd like to tweak the lyrics a bit," said Tara.

A collective groan went up from all the members of Wizard Monkey Breath Scares the Horses.

"No, seriously!" said Tara. "I think if I did it would help Chloe's breathing." She paused. "I don't want to alter the riff though," she added, looking at Ben. "It's perfect just as it is."

Ben scowled at her and then grinned. "I guess I'll just have to keep practising then," he told her. "I'll get it right in the end."

"I'm sure it's only us that notice," Danny told him. "It's not as if you're out of tune or anything like that. It's just that you hesitate slightly longer than you should on that one note."

"I'm glad you're all so determined to make this song the best it can be," said Judge Jim, in a very pleased voice. "Let's hear all about the changes you're proposin', Tara. Then we'll have a run-through."

A Frantic Week

*

The run-through went very well, but there were other things to attend to before they left for Italy in ten days' time. The stylist Mrs. Sharkey had engaged, to get their look just right, wanted to see the band several times before they travelled. Also, their stage clothes had to be cleaned and checked over for any imperfections before they were packed.

"Is it all right?" Chloe asked, as the stylist cast a critical eye over her dress. The stylist nodded and Chloe breathed a sigh of contentment. It made Chloe feel very special, for the school to have had a dress made especially for the competition. She was sure that wearing the beautiful, sequinned, sky-blue dress had helped her performance. The way it shimmered and flowed around as she moved about the stage was magical. It made her feel like the star she had always wanted to be. So it wouldn't do for it to be anything less than perfect.

Mr. Penardos, the dance teacher, wanted to come along to rehearsals. It was vital to position the band members correctly onstage. Although of course Danny wouldn't be dancing, Chloe and the guitarists would be moving around the stage, and it was important to choreograph their moves so they looked just right. Although they'd discussed all this before the first leg of the competition, it needed talking over again. The school had invested a lot of time and money in this enterprise and everything had to be perfect for the final.

Chloe began to wonder how she'd ever had time for ordinary school lessons in the past. She'd always prepared thoroughly for performances, but that wasn't *anything* compared to all the work they had put in for this one. However, they *were* going to be representing their country. And surely nothing was more important than that!

The days raced along, as there was so much to do, and in no time at all, it was the evening before the trip.

"I can't believe I'm going tomorrow!" said Chloe, feeling both excited and nervous at the same time.

They were going to be away for three nights, and Pop and Lolly had plenty of suggestions for the sort of clothes Chloe and Tara should take with them.

"I'll need clothes for sightseeing as well as rehearsals," said Chloe.

"And you must remember that you will probably be filmed for TV while you're sightseeing," added Pop.

"Help!" said Chloe, looking at the contents of her wardrobe in despair.

"None of that bothers me," said Tara. "I'll just wear my usual clothes." She took an armful of her trademark black jeans and tops out of her cupboard and started to select a few.

Chloe and Lolly looked at each other and sighed. It was impossible to get Tara to wear anything except black.

"It does seem a shame—" began Chloe, but Pop interrupted.

"No. Actually it'll probably look really cool, with Tara all brooding in black next to you in lovely colours," she mused. "Think of it," Pop went on. "The sad artist, only able to express herself through her songwriting, even while sightseeing."

"Rubbish!" said Tara, throwing a pair of rolled-up socks at Pop.

"Stop it, Pop," said Lolly. "We're supposed to be helping Chloe."

"You're right," Pop agreed, bounding over to Chloe's wardrobe. "It'll be hot in Italy," she told Chloe. "So you'll need loose clothes and a hat. Pale colours are best too," she added, glancing at Tara.

"Unless you can cope with the heat, like me," Tara added with a sniff.

Chloe sighed. "I'll *definitely* need a hat," she agreed, wishing she was as seasoned a traveller as Tara and the twins. Tara's parents were always jetting off round the world and Tara joined them when she could. She had even flown back to school from Africa on her own last year! On the other hand, Chloe knew that Tara hated not seeing much of her parents.

"Take plenty of loose tops," advised Lolly. "Then you can change as often as you like and always look cool. Have you got any thin cotton trousers?"

Chloe shook her head. "Only some really old ones," she admitted.

"Try these on," said Pop, tossing a couple of her pairs onto Chloe's bed. "They'll be so much cooler than jeans."

"And why don't you take a couple of my silk tops?" suggested Lolly. "They'll be cool, and just right when you want to look glamorous!"

Chloe's special sky-blue dress had been folded with tissue, and given to her all ready to put in her case. As soon as all the rest of her things were packed, she put it carefully on the top and closed the case.

"I'm going to put some of these competition stickers on my suitcase," said Chloe. "They'll help to jazz it up a bit."

"Good idea," enthused Pop, looking at the large, brightly coloured stickers the competition organizers had sent to publicize the event. "They'll make your luggage easy to find at the airport baggage hall and they'll tell everyone how important you are too!"

Tara shook her head. "I suppose it's fair enough to

put them on your case," she said, glancing at Chloe's vinyl luggage. "But I'm not going to spoil mine."

Chloe and Lolly exchanged glances. Tara's bag was black leather, and looked very expensive. But Chloe didn't mind. She'd far rather not have to fret about looking after designer luggage. She grinned at Lolly and handed her a couple of stickers.

"You put some on that side," she urged her. "And I'll do this side. I think there's one to go on the handle too!"

By the time Mrs. Pinto, their housemistress, came in to turn out the light, Chloe and Tara were all packed and ready to go.

"The minibus will be coming for you at five in the morning," she reminded the girls. "So get to sleep straight away. It'll be a long day tomorrow."

Chloe lay down and closed her eyes, but it was impossible to sleep. Her eyes kept flying open again, because so many thoughts were whirling round her head. Would she be travel-sick? She'd never been in a plane before. Would she and Tara get on okay? Tara could be rather grumpy, and Chloe felt in need of a good friend.

Chloe hadn't felt homesick for ages. She had quickly got used to being without her family during term time, but now she was missing them a lot. She didn't really like the idea of flying off to a foreign country without them. If she'd been able to give them a goodbye hug it would have been better, but that was impossible. And a long phone call earlier in the evening wasn't really the same.

Chloe hoped the soundcheck would go well too. It would be awful if there were any technical hitches. She had suffered problems with a soundcheck once before, when she had been performing at the Rising Stars concert on television, and that had been *terrible*. All these worries were keeping her awake, and the others weren't helping her get to sleep either.

"Passport?" muttered Tara.

"In my bag," replied Chloe.

"Phone charger?" asked Lolly.

"Yes," Chloe assured her.

"Pocket money?"

"Yes, Pop."

"Judge Jim's got the plane tickets, hasn't he?" asked Lolly.

But there was no answer. In spite of being sure she'd never sleep, tiredness had overwhelmed Chloe and she was already dreaming of tomorrow.

3 A Long Journey

Very early the next morning Chloe and Tara were in the dining room, trying to eat the breakfast that had been left out for them. Pop and Lolly had insisted on getting up to say goodbye, but they had gone straight back to bed after giving the girls a big hug and wishing them all the best.

"I'm not really hungry," Chloe told Danny, pushing her cereal round her bowl.

"Me neither," admitted Danny.

"You'll be hungry later," warned Tara, buttering a piece of toast. "You ought to try and eat something."

"You sound like my mum," complained Ben.

Just then Judge Jim arrived with Mr. and Mrs.

Player. Chloe was pleased that Mr. Player, her singing teacher, was coming with them. And his wife was going to look after the two girls. Chloe had never met her before, but if she was as nice as her husband they were bound to get on well.

Everyone said hello, and Mrs. Player was introduced to the students. She sat down next to Chloe and Tara.

"How are you feeling?" she asked them.

"A bit nervous," admitted Chloe, not mentioning her homesickness.

"I'm not surprised," said Mrs. Player, with a sympathetic smile. "But I hope you'll enjoy the trip. Don't worry if you can't eat," she added, looking at Chloe's unfinished cereal. "I expect we'll be offered something after we take off."

On the bus, Chloe would have liked to sit with Danny, but he was one of the last to get on, and Tara had already plonked herself down next to Chloe.

"Because you haven't been abroad before I'm going to be looking after you," Tara announced. "So that you enjoy the trip *and* sing so well that we win."

Chloe thought Tara was joking, but when she looked at her she could see that Tara really meant it. "Thanks," she said, feeling quite touched. "I'll do my best."

"I know you will," agreed Tara. "And so will I."

They smiled at each other, and Chloe began to feel much happier.

At the airport they didn't have to queue too long to check in their bags. Chloe watched her suitcase disappear and clutched her hand luggage tightly. Once they had gone through to the departure lounge, Mr. Player found a good spot for them to wait. Chloe and Danny spent ages watching the planes taking off and landing through the large observation window.

"I've only been on a plane once before," Danny admitted as they watched a huge jet take off.

"Did you like it?" she replied. "I haven't *ever* flown."

"I was too young to remember," he said. "But I think it's exciting. Don't you?"

"I *think* so," said Chloe uncertainly.

But as soon as they got on board Chloe forgot all her worries. It *was* exciting. Tara let her have the window seat, and explained all about the seat belt, and stowing baggage. It was fun eating the meal, which came in little plastic pots and dishes. By the time they started to make their descent, Chloe was beginning to feel quite relaxed about travelling. She looked out as they came in to land and was thrilled to see all the houses, roads and cars rushing up to greet them.

As they taxied up to the terminal building and stopped, everyone started to undo their seat belts, and gather their luggage. Tara got up and Chloe queued behind her to disembark. Suddenly, a sea of uncertainty threatened to overwhelm her. She had landed in a foreign country, where she didn't know anyone except her fellow students and teachers. She'd only just arrived, but her homesickness was really getting to her. She hadn't been able to hug her mum and dad and little brother goodbye, and, more than anything, she wished they were with her now. After all, what if everything went wrong? How could she bear it if she made a mess of her performance? And she might get lost, or fall ill... anything could happen!

A Long Journey

"All right, Chloe?" It was Mrs. Player. Chloe nodded and Mrs. Player smiled. "You'll be fine," she reassured her. "And if you have any worries at all just come and tell me. Even if it's that my husband is pushing you too hard. I know what he can be like!"

"Stick with me and don't wander off," warned Tara, as they entered the terminal building through a long tunnel. "It can be a bit manic in these airports."

Chloe had no intention of wandering anywhere! She was happy to rely on Tara, however bossy she was. At least Tara – the seasoned traveller – knew what she was doing.

The noise in the baggage collection hall was tremendous, and there were people everywhere, pushing shiny trolleys or carrying huge bags and suitcases. Tara pushed imperiously through the crush and made her way to the correct carousel for their flight.

"It's easy when you know how," she told Chloe briskly, pulling her suitcase off the carousel. "The flight number is displayed up there. You just have to look."

She tapped her foot impatiently, while they waited for the other bags to arrive. Chloe spent the time gazing all around her. There was so much to see, but she wished her suitcase would hurry up and appear, she was desperate for the loo and she hadn't noticed one nearby.

"It's over there," said Tara, when Chloe asked. "Come on, I'll take you," she added, seeing Chloe's worried face.

"But what about my suitcase?" asked Chloe.

"Don't worry. It'll appear soon," Tara told her. "There's still a load of baggage coming in from the plane. If your case arrives before we get back it'll just keep going round on the carousel until we pick it up."

Even the loos were different from the ones Chloe was used to. It took her a few seconds to work out how to flush, and how to turn on the tap over the hand basin. While she dried her hands, Chloe listened to all the voices, speaking words in a language she didn't understand. It was a bit scary, being so far from home, but it was also very exciting.

"Come on then," laughed Tara.

"What are you laughing at?" asked Chloe, as they made their way back to the others.

"You!" said Tara. "You look as if you've been let loose in a sweet shop and don't know what to try first."

Chloe started to feel cross. Then she laughed too. "It's all so new, and different," she admitted. "And fun," she added.

"Good," said Tara. "But wait until you try some real Italian food. That will be even *more* fun."

Everyone was waiting in a group with their luggage, but Chloe's still hadn't appeared. And now there were only a few bags left to be collected.

"Are you sure none of those is yours?" asked Mrs. Player, when the girls told her about the missing suitcase.

Chloe stared hard at the half-dozen cases still on the carousel. "No," she told Mrs. Player miserably. "Mine had lots of competition stickers all over it."

"And you definitely checked it in at the other end?"

Chloe nodded. She was beginning to feel breathless

with panic. Not only did her case have all her spare clothes, and the lovely ones Pop and Lolly had lent her, it also held her beautiful sky-blue dress and silver shoes for the competition. She *had* to find it!

Everyone waited while Mr. and Mrs. Player went with Chloe to report the missing case. They had to fill out several forms, and somehow Chloe got the feeling that the officials weren't terribly interested in her lost case.

"Well, that's all we can do for now," said Mrs. Player, putting her arm round Chloe. "Try not to worry. These things happen."

"But what will I do if it doesn't turn up?" asked Chloe tearfully. "How can I possibly perform without my dress?"

They had only just arrived in Italy, and already the trip was turning into a disaster.

4 An Amazing Venue

Chloe was too worried about her missing suitcase to enjoy the hotel room she was sharing with Tara. It was a pity, because it was the first time she'd stayed in a hotel, and the room was great, with an en suite bathroom and a lovely little balcony.

Mrs. Player had taken Chloe to the airport shop and bought her a toothbrush and some underwear, but, although she was grateful, Chloe wasn't reassured. She wanted her *own* things, and watching Tara unpack just made her feel worse.

But once the hotel and the airport had been informed of the missing case there wasn't anything anyone could do but wait. Meanwhile, the band had to go to inspect the competition venue, which was on the outskirts of the city. A shuttle bus service had been laid on by the concert organizers, so that everyone involved could get to and from the venue, and a bus was expected in the next few minutes.

Luckily, the bus wasn't too full when it arrived, because lots of people wanted to get on. There were teachers and band members from several countries staying in Chloe's hotel, and everyone wanted their first look at the venue. Chloe gazed out at the busy city streets as the bus nosed its way through the traffic. It was exciting seeing all the shop signs written in a foreign language, and they passed a couple of ancient ruins that Chloe was sure she had seen in her history book. It was all so interesting that she started to relax a little. After all, worrying wouldn't help, and her case was sure to turn up soon. She might as well enjoy this trip of a lifetime as much as she could.

It didn't take too long to reach the large arena where the event was to be staged. Chloe and Tara exchanged glances as the huge dome covering the venue came into sight. Every member of Wizard Monkey Breath Scares the Horses looked nervous at the sight of it. The bus dropped them at the main entrance and pulled away. On every side there were huge expanses of car park, and the building seemed almost as big as a football stadium!

Once inside, even Mr. Player appeared lost for words. The stage looked miles away from the back of the auditorium and it was vast. Huge video screens stood on both sides, and the lighting and sound crews working onstage were like ants.

It was Mrs. Player who broke the silence. "Well," she said calmly. "I've never seen anything like it. Shall we go a bit closer to the stage?"

Judge Jim laughed. "That's the spirit!" he told her.

They made their way along the main aisle. "It's all so shiny!" said Danny.

He was right. The arena was very modern, a bit like the hotel they were staying in. There was lots of silvery metalwork and reflective walls on all sides. They had got about halfway to the stage when suddenly all the walls lit up with bright, electric colours of pink and blue.

"Wow!" gasped Chloe.

"They're doing a lighting check," said Mr. Player.

Banks of light shone up from the floor, illuminating the auditorium. As they watched, the colours changed several times. Overhead lights came on too, until Chloe felt she was standing in multicoloured sunlight.

"I thought it was the stage that would be lit, not the seats!" she said.

"They're probably just testing everything," Mr. Player answered.

"Good afternoon!" a stranger's voice interrupted them.

No one had noticed the dark-haired woman approaching them. She was elegantly dressed, in a silk suit, and had a big smile on her face.

"I am Silvia, one of your hosts for this event," she told them. "Could you tell me the country you are representing and the name of your band, please?"

"We're from the UK," said Judge Jim, smiling back

at the woman. "And this is the junior rock band, Wizard Monkey Breath Scares the Horses."

"I thought so," Silvia said. They all shook hands and Silvia led them towards the stage. "You have an interesting band name," she told Chloe.

"That was my idea," said Tara.

"Ah," said Silvia. "Well I think it will be hard for the judges to understand what the name means."

"We're not sure what it means either!" said Ben. Ed nudged him and Silvia laughed.

"It is the music that is important," she reassured them.

Silvia led the way and soon Chloe and the others were climbing the steps at the front of the stage. Once they were up there, Chloe could see that although the stage looked huge, the part marked out for the performers wasn't too enormous after all.

Danny made for the drum kit and ran his fingers lightly over all the drum skins and cymbals, just like he always did at home. "I've brought my own snare drum," he told Silvia. "Will that be okay?"

Battle of the Bands

"Of course," she replied. "Bring it tomorrow for your rehearsal. It will be booked in and given a code number so the technicians will know which song it is for. You also will be given the code number so you can get it back at the end of the competition."

"You sound very well organized," said Mrs. Player.

"We have to be," said Silvia. "With so many countries entering bands and so many performers we have to make sure everything runs smoothly. And we must fit it all into four hours, which is quite a challenge!"

"I love the floor!" said Chloe. It was made up of mirrored tiles and was beautifully smooth to walk on. Chloe was beginning to imagine how it might be to perform here and her nervousness was turning into a jumpy excitement. She wished she could have a rehearsal right now, but knew that they weren't scheduled to use the stage until the next day.

"This whole arena is very special," Silvia told Chloe. "It was designed by one of our most famous architects."

But Silvia didn't have time to show them any more. She had spotted another group arriving and needed to welcome them. "Feel free to wander around as much as you like," she told Judge Jim. "Here are your badges and key passes, which will get you into the backstage areas you need to access. Please wear them at all times. Good luck with the competition, and if you need any information just ask at the front desk."

"Well," said Mr. Player. "I think it's going to be fine. What a venue! I wish I'd had the chance to sing in a place like this."

Mr. Player had been a famous recording artist, before retiring to teach at Rockley Park. Chloe's mum even had one of his albums.

"Shall we go and check out backstage?" suggested Ed.

"Good idea," agreed Judge Jim. "I'd like to see what sort of instrument store they've got, an' meet the sound engineer if possible."

They hung their passes round their necks. When they reached the door to the backstage area, they found that the passes worked like the hotel room cards to let them in.

"Fantastic!" said Ben, looking very impressed.

Backstage there were lots of rooms. Some were for rehearsals, and others were dressing rooms for costume fittings, and there was even a large canteen.

"I need to take the costumes to the wardrobe department," said Mrs. Player. "Do you girls want to come with me?"

"I will," said Chloe quickly. "Maybe the airport will have sent my suitcase here."

Mrs. Player looked surprised. "Why would you think they'd do that?" she asked.

Chloe blushed. "I stuck lots of those competition stickers on the outside," she said. "The venue address is on them all."

"Oh." Mrs. Player looked concerned. "I hope your case *doesn't* turn up here. The place is so vast it could end up anywhere in the building. Did you put the hotel address on the luggage labels you were given?"

Chloe nodded hastily. "I'm sorry I put the stickers on my case," she apologized, feeling very unworldly.

"Try not to worry too much," said Judge Jim kindly.

An Amazing Venue

"You weren't to know that your case was goin' to go missin'. If it ends up here I expect it'll be delivered to the front desk, and they'll keep it safe if we tell them how importan' it is."

"Do you mind if I go with the boys?" asked Tara, looking longingly at the guitars being carried by some members of another band.

"Of course not," said Chloe. She knew that Tara wasn't interested in the costumes.

"We'll see you at the front desk in about twenty minutes," said Mr. Player.

Chloe and Mrs. Player headed for the costume room. There were already racks of numbered clothes that were pressed and ready for the performers. Finally, they found the wardrobe mistress and gave her the band name and nationality.

"*Si*. Your place is here," the woman told them, pointing to a rack over by the wall. "This code number must be on every item." She handed Chloe some sticky labels to put on the plastic garment covers.

"Here we are," said Mrs. Player, hanging the clothes

on the correct rail. "Make sure those labels stick well on the covers, Chloe. We don't want any more clothes going astray, do we?"

"No," said Chloe, miserably. She looked at all the gorgeous, plastic-wrapped clothes on the rails. Whatever was she going to do if her suitcase didn't turn up?

The woman in charge came over. She counted the number of hangers Mrs. Player had added to the rail, and then looked at her notebook. "Eight pieces?" she asked, tapping the book. "Not ten?"

"There will be ten pieces booked in eventually," said Mrs. Player. "A top and trousers for each musician, and then Chloe's dress and shoes, but her case has gone missing for the moment."

"You haven't seen a stray suitcase, have you?" asked Chloe hopefully, but the woman didn't understand.

"Eight pieces," the woman said again, and showed them the page. "Ten pieces." Unlike Silvia, her English wasn't good and, although Mrs. Player tried speaking her few words of Italian, they didn't get much further.

Chloe had a lump in her throat. It was the sort of lump that she knew very well would lead to tears if she wasn't careful, and so she tried very hard to ignore it. She wasn't a baby. She mustn't cry over a dress, even the very special sky-blue dress. She did her best not to think of the glorious bright-blue silk that flowed around her like water when she wore it, and the sparkling sequins. Would she ever be able to sing as well without it?

"Come on," said Mrs. Player. "Let's go and report the missing case to the front desk."

They hurried back into the auditorium and through to the front desk. They had to wait in a queue and while they were waiting the others joined them. Chloe's friends were all sympathetic, but they couldn't help looking excited. They were having a wonderful time. Their expressions just made her feel worse, and before she could stop herself tears started sliding down Chloe's cheeks.

5 Disaster

Chloe did her best to stop crying, but it was no use. All the stress of the journey, and nervousness over the competition was difficult enough, but worry about her suitcase – especially the dress – was overwhelming.

"What if it doesn't turn up?" she kept asking through her sobs.

"Relax," Tara told her. "The case has to be somewhere. I'm sure you'll get it in time."

"But what if I don't? There isn't anything else I can wear." Chloe couldn't imagine having to appear in the simple pair of cotton trousers that she had on now. The idea was horrific. She knew that every country would have gone overboard to make their bands look as glitzy as possible. Some of the clothes she'd seen hanging up looked *wonderful*. It wasn't just the playing and singing, although that was the most important thing about the competition. The whole package really mattered. How they looked was vitally important, which was why Rockley Park had employed a stylist. Now, all her hard work was ruined.

But it wasn't any good crying, and so while Chloe conquered her tears, Mrs. Player reported the missing suitcase to the front desk. The official was very sympathetic and promised to let them know if it turned up.

"There. We've done everything we can," said Mrs. Player to Chloe.

"The next thing is to go back to the hotel," said Mr. Player. "I expect it will probably be there when we return."

But, back at the hotel, there was still no sign of Chloe's case, and so Mrs. Player took Chloe out into the hot streets to buy her a few clothes, while Tara and the boys went for a swim in the hotel pool.

Battle of the Bands

Under any other circumstances Chloe would have loved having clothes bought for her in Italy. There was a large store almost opposite the hotel, where they found Chloe a couple of T-shirts, a skirt, and a new swimsuit, so she could use the pool. But although the shop had an excellent selection of clothes, it had nothing that either of them thought suitable for the concert.

"You can't wear chain-store clothes for such an important event," said Mrs. Player. "After all, you'll be representing our country."

Chloe agreed. The sky-blue dress was a one-off. Chain-store clothes could never replace it.

Back at the hotel Mr. and Mrs. Player did all they could to find Chloe's missing suitcase. They spoke to the manager of the hotel, telephoned the airline again several times, and rang the venue in case there was any news there, but the case seemed to have vanished into thin air. Chloe had calmed down since her tears at the competition venue, but she didn't really feel calm inside. Her stomach kept churning, she felt sick, and her heart was racing.

What she really wanted to do was hide in her room and cry, but that was neither sensible nor possible. The hotel had organized a special meal for all the competitors staying with them, and Chloe was expected to attend, however bad she felt. She had a shower and put on the new skirt and T-shirt, but they didn't make her feel much better.

"Come on, Chloe," said Tara. "We ought to go down to the dining room. Maybe your suitcase will turn up while we're eating."

Chloe nodded, trying to put on a brave face. "You hate all this fuss, don't you?" she said.

"Yep," admitted Tara cheerfully. "But that doesn't mean I'm not sympathetic," she added hurriedly. "Do you want to borrow anything of mine for tonight? We're a similar size. "

"Not really," Chloe told her, with a wan smile. "But it's kind of you to offer."

"Why don't you just go out again, find a better shop, and buy a new dress for the performance?" Tara suggested. They were on their way to the lift. Chloe stopped walking and looked at Tara in disbelief.

"How could I possibly do that?" she asked miserably.

"It's simple!" said Tara. "Just go shopping instead of on the official sightseeing trip tomorrow morning. You should easily find a shop that sells the right sort of stuff by the time we're due to rehearse in the afternoon."

"It might be easy for you, but not for me," Chloe told her angrily. "To start with there's the problem of money. I already owe Mrs. Player for the clothes she's just bought me, and what about Pop and Lolly's things that have gone missing? I'll have to offer to replace them. Then I wouldn't know where to go for such a special dress, and also I can't speak Italian."

"Well pardon me for trying to help!" said Tara. She strode to the lift in a huff and Chloe followed, feeling even worse than before. Tara was well travelled and confident. She wouldn't let something like a lost dress put her out. She *would* simply march off to the nearest suitable shop and buy another one. Chloe felt like a misfit. She was beginning to wish she'd never come.

If only Pop and Lolly were here to help it wouldn't be so bad, but at the moment she felt really alone.

Downstairs, the dining room was full of students from different countries, and there was a photographer taking lots of pictures. Chloe could see Pink Toffee, the all-girl band from Sedge Combe School that had beaten The Rockley Five. They were all dressed in pink skirts with pink-and-brown-striped T-shirts, and were chattering happily together. Chloe was in no mood to be impressed. *Trust them to show off by wearing matching clothes even at supper,* she thought. She knew it was uncharitable of her, but she was too depressed about her own problem to feel kind.

The students weren't allowed to sit just where they wanted. There were names at every place setting and it took a while for everyone to find their places. Chloe had to sit opposite a friendly looking boy from Spain, who spoke no English. On her left there was a Polish boy, talking quickly to the girl next to him. On the other side, an Italian girl with long, dark hair and laughing eyes was talking to Danny.

Battle of the Bands

Chloe had a look round for the rest of her band. Ed and Ben were on the same table as a couple of the girls from Pink Toffee. They all seemed to be having a great time. Tara was chatting to a boy with long dark hair. Only Chloe was feeling left out.

Chloe knew it was rude, but she pulled her mobile out of her bag. She couldn't spend the whole meal smiling wordlessly at the Spanish boy, however nice he looked. She needed to talk to someone, and if she couldn't do that, the next best thing was texting. So she sent a long text to Lolly, telling her what had happened. She apologized for losing the twins' clothes, and offered to replace them. Then she put the mobile back in her pocket and concentrated on her food. Tara had been right about real Italian food: it was delicious.

Before Chloe had finished her pasta, her phone vibrated and she knew she'd got a text. She shovelled down the last few forkfuls of her food and grabbed her mobile. Sure enough it was from Lolly.

Has anyone phoned Mrs. Sharkey yet? it said. *We'll*

look into flying some of our things over for you. And there are good shops nearby. The school ought to pay. Speak to Mrs. Player. Whatever you do, don't panic. It'll be all right. And don't worry about our things being lost. We have far too many clothes anyway.

"Excuse me. Are you all right?" It was the girl who had been talking to Danny. "My name is Caterina." Her English seemed good. No wonder Danny had been talking to her so much.

"My name's Chloe."

"I just want to say I am sure your luggage will arrive soon. I am sorry you have trouble."

Chloe realized that news about her missing case must have travelled through the contestants like wildfire. It was nice of Caterina to sympathize, though.

"Thanks," Chloe said gratefully.

"Danny is your boyfriend?" Caterina smiled at Chloe questioningly.

"No, no, he's not my boyfriend," replied Chloe, feeling amused and embarrassed at the same time. "We're friends. In the same band."

"So he says," Caterina agreed. "I am in a singing band only. No instruments. We are called I Gatti Selvaggi. In English you would say The Wildcats."

"That's a good name," said Chloe, happy to think about something other than her misfortune for the moment. "Especially as you are a Cat too."

Catarina looked confused. "Sorry?"

"Your name," explained Chloe. "In England, Cat is short for Caterina. So you really are a wild Cat!"

Caterina laughed. "Not too wild I hope!" she said. "In Italian, cat is *gatti* so it is not so obvious for me, but I like it. I will tell my friends I must be called Cat from now on! I will wish hard for your luggage to arrive very soon," she added, before turning back to Danny.

During the next course the photographer reached Chloe. She tried to smile for him, but was sure her effort had been rather lopsided. When he pointed his camera at Danny, Cat leaned in and put her head against his. The photographer laughed. He took a couple of pictures and said a few words to Cat in Italian. Now it was her turn to laugh. She took hold of

Chloe's arm and pulled her in close too, so the photographer could take a picture of all three of them. Then she threw her arms round Danny and gave him a kiss on the cheek.

The photographer moved on and Chloe sneaked a look at Danny. He was blushing, but obviously rather pleased. It looked as if Danny might have found himself an Italian girlfriend!

Before the meal ended, Chloe had another text from Lolly. It was a list of shops and their addresses.

It's all very well for Lolly, thought Chloe crossly. *She hasn't got to find all these shops!*

She looked beside her, where Cat was deep in a giggling conversation with Danny again. It was on the tip of Chloe's tongue to ask Cat for her help. It would be wonderful if Cat could join Chloe in her quest for a new dress. But they were all on such a tight schedule. There was no way Cat would be allowed to chase across the city looking for clothes. And it wouldn't be fair to ask. Oh why did life have to be so difficult?

6 Friends

The meal was coming to an end and people were beginning to get up and mingle again. Cat turned to Chloe and smiled. "Maybe we can be friends?" she suggested.

"Yes." Chloe smiled back. At least people were being nice to her. Danny got up from the table with the girls, and Cat linked arms with them both. But before they could go anywhere Ed and Ben arrived.

"Hey!" said Ben, with a broad grin. "Who's your girlfriend, Danny?"

"We saw you having your photograph taken," added Ed, making a kissing sound.

Everyone laughed.

"This is Caterina," said Danny mildly. "She's a singer with The Wildcats."

Cat pursed her lips and blew a kiss to Ed, who blushed. She laughed and winked at Chloe. "Your British boys are so funny," she told her. "Are you all going to the disco later?" she added to Ben. "Maybe we can dance, yes? Or maybe you will be with those Pink Toffee girls. No?" She gave him a slow smile and now it was Ben's turn to blush. "But for you the first dance, please?" she added, looking more seriously at Danny.

Danny shrugged uncomfortably, but looked pleased.

Before he could reply Judge Jim arrived. He smiled politely to Cat, then turned to the band. "We're havin' a meetin' in Mr. Player's room now."

Up in the Players' room the students all squeezed onto the balcony to catch the slight breeze.

"I wanted to tell you about a phone call I've had from the Principal," explained Judge Jim. "She said Chloe should go an' buy somethin' else to wear for the performance, in case her suitcase doesn't turn up. I think you already have a list of suggested shops," he added.

"Yes," Chloe said. "Lolly sent them to me. But I can't go on my own!"

"No one is expecting you to," said Mrs. Player. "I'm here to look after you girls. We can go together first thing in the morning."

"Do you want me to come?" asked Tara.

"You don't have to," said Mrs. Player, "if you'd rather go on the sightseeing trip."

"Please come!" begged Chloe. "I'd really like you to." At least Tara was the same age as Chloe, and you never knew; lurking underneath all those black clothes there might be some fashion sense. At least she might have more idea than Mrs. Player.

Tara sighed. "Okay," she agreed. "I've already seen most of the sights. I was here a couple of years ago on holiday."

"Thank you *so* much, Tara," said Chloe gratefully.

She sighed with relief. Even if her case didn't turn up it looked as if things would be all right. They were bound to find something suitable for her to wear, and

Chloe was sure Tara would back her up if Mrs. Player was tempted by anything awful.

"The other thing is just to remind you that even at things like the disco tonight, you're still representing your country," said Mr. Player.

"We don' want to spoil your fun," said Judge Jim. "You deserve it after winnin' through to get here. But be sensible, and don't stay up too late. You've got a busy day tomorrow."

"I'll keep an eye on them," said Mr. Player. "I fancy another coffee anyway."

When they went back downstairs there were students all over the place, sitting in the reception area, lounging in the café and wandering up and down the corridor as well as in the disco. The Pink Toffee girls came up to say hello to Ben and Ed, and they all decided to go to the café for a drink.

"I'm Suzy, and this is Abby and Keira," said the nearest Pink Toffee. They had all changed and were wearing short, pink net skirts over toffee-coloured leggings. Chloe thought they looked ridiculous.

The boys went to get the drinks while the girls found seats. "Isn't this competition exciting!" said Suzy to Tara.

Tara grunted. Chloe could tell that Tara disapproved of the Pink Toffees. Everything about them was totally alien to Tara.

Abby looked at Chloe's plain T-shirt and skirt and smoothed down her silly net skirt ostentatiously.

"Isn't it awful about your lost case!" said Suzy to Chloe. "I was so sorry when Ed told us about it. All your clothes and toiletries – and your competition dress! You must be, like, totally *crushed* by it."

Chloe didn't want anyone thinking she was *crushed*. And she couldn't help feeling that even if Suzy felt genuinely sorry for her, she had enjoyed the gossip, too. "It would be nice to have my toiletries," Chloe admitted. "But it'll be okay," she told Suzy, crossing her fingers out of sight. "I'm going shopping for a new dress tomorrow. And Italian fashion is so *cool*. I'm really looking forward to it."

Much later, in their room, Chloe and Tara were just

about to turn out their light and go to sleep when there was a knock on their door. Chloe went to answer it. Outside were Cat, Suzy and several other girls from different bands. Cat held out a box to Chloe.

"Some of us get things to make up for lost luggage," she told Chloe. "I hope is okay."

"Thank you!" said Chloe, feeling very touched. "That's really kind of you."

"Not just us," Cat told her. "Lots of people want to help with horrible problem. There is card here with all names. Now we must go. Good night."

Chloe closed the door and sat on the end of Tara's bed, hugging the box. They both peered in. There were all sorts of toiletries, some make-up and a hairbrush, as well as a lovely scarf.

"People are so kind," Chloe said to Tara. "And with so many wishing me well I'm *sure* tomorrow will be fine."

"You wait," said Tara. "We'll find you the best dress in all Italy."

"Yes!" agreed Chloe, her eyes shining. "I bet we will."

7 Shopping

In the morning, the hotel ordered a taxi and once Mrs. Player had made sure that the suitcase still hadn't turned up, they set off on their shopping trip. The driver knew a bit of English and was very helpful. Chloe and Tara sat in the back, while Mrs. Player showed him the list of shops Lolly had texted Chloe.

"Okay," he said, starting the engine. "I take you first to these three shops. They are," he waved an arm, "all over city. Then we go famous shopping area where the other shops are. I leave you there and," he pointed at the phone, "you telephone when you are finish."

The first two shops weren't any good. They didn't have anything to fit Chloe at all. The third shop had two dresses that fitted her well, but neither of them was right.

"I can't wear that!" said Chloe, when Tara picked out a spectacular ball gown in crimson taffeta. "It wouldn't go with yours and the boys' clothes at all." She looked at the huge, flounced skirt and shuddered. "I'd look like a Christmas tree decoration!" The lady in the shop looked most put out and they beat a hasty retreat.

The taxi driver looked at Chloe's doleful face and smiled. "Next is the best," he told her. "Many, many shops for you to choose. I show you." They entered a wide, modern street, full of shoppers and slow-moving traffic. He drew to a halt with a flourish, right in the middle of a bus stop. Several cars honked their horns at him but he ignored them.

"Go down there," he told them. "And you will find what you look for. I am certain." He gave Mrs. Player a small card. "When you finish, ring this number," he said. "I will come and collect. Okay? *Ciao!*" He roared away in a haze of diesel fumes and left them standing on the pavement.

"Well," said Mrs. Player brightly. "Let's go and have a look, shall we?"

Some of the shops were very intimidating. A couple even had security locks on the doors and they had to ring a bell to be let in. Chloe's knowledge of euros was a bit hazy, but the price tags in these shops seemed to have enormous numbers on them, and the clothes certainly looked expensive. Unlike the places Chloe usually went to, there were very few clothes in these shops, and it was impossible to browse. At first the assistants seemed to think that Chloe and Tara were in the wrong place, but once Mrs. Player explained about Chloe's problem to one of the assistants, the women couldn't have been more helpful.

"No dresses in sky blue," said the assistant, who spoke impeccable English. "Blue isn't one of our colours this season. Taupe is in, and mustard, but that's rather an old colour for you to carry off." She looked at Chloe and Chloe had to agree. In fact, she thought all the colours on offer were hideous, but didn't like to say so.

Unfortunately, Mrs. Player didn't realize how she felt, and pointed to a pale beige shift dress. "That looks as if it might fit you," she said. "Why don't you try it on?"

It was the last thing in the world Chloe wanted to do, but somehow she found herself being bundled into a changing room with the dress. The shop assistant hovered outside and, as soon as Chloe emerged, she started pinning the dress in various places to make it fit better.

Chloe had to admit that the fabric felt good next to her skin, but the colour was horrible.

"That looks okay!" said Tara. "It would look fantastic with some strappy sandals."

She was right, but Chloe still didn't like the colour. It simply wasn't the sort of dress she had envisaged herself wearing. "I'm sorry," she told Mrs. Player in a small voice. "I really don't like it."

"Well it's the best thing we've seen so far," said Mrs. Player, sounding harassed. "We'd better see if they'll reserve it for us, in case we don't find anything you like better."

The shop assistant took their details and agreed to keep the dress for the day, but Chloe felt desperate at the thought of having to go back and buy it. She didn't want a pale brown dress. She wanted something that would make her feel great, and that dress made her feel lumpy and graceless.

They tried loads of other shops. They found one amazing shoe shop that had all sorts of styles and colours. Chloe loved them all, but there was no point in buying shoes before they had a dress. At least they knew they could go back there eventually.

They were all getting hot and fed up, so Mrs. Player suggested they stop for an ice cream while she phoned the hotel and the airport again to check that Chloe's suitcase hadn't turned up. "They've got my mobile number, so should let us know, but it won't hurt to check," she said.

"Why don't we go back and get that beige one?" suggested Tara, when it was clear that the case still hadn't turned up. "Then at least you've got something."

Mrs. Player looked at her and Chloe swallowed nervously. She was putting Mrs. Player and Tara to an awful lot of bother, but even so, she couldn't bring herself to agree.

"I just don't..." She hesitated. She didn't want to sound ungrateful, or spoiled, but there was no way to explain how she felt. "It's just so...*brown*," she told them, feeling awful.

"Does it matter whether you like it or not?" asked Tara bluntly. "After all, it's just to sing one song in. Surely you can live with that?"

"It would be like asking you to perform wearing a frilly pink dress," Chloe told her.

Tara looked both startled and appalled. "Never!" she said, sounding quite shaken. "I see what you mean. I wasn't that keen on wearing blue, like we have to for the performance, but at least it's bearable. Okay, no brown dress. Besides, it's almost toffee colour. You might get mistaken for a member of Pink Toffee. Imagine that!"

Mrs. Player sighed. "I don't think we can do any

more now," she told them, after looking at her watch. "We need to get back so you can have lunch before your rehearsal. I'll ring the taxi, and when we get back I'll make a last effort to find the case. We'll have a small window tomorrow when we can collect the beige dress if we have to, and buy some shoes to go with it. Don't worry. It will be a last resort, but you must accept that if the sky-blue dress doesn't turn up, we have very little choice."

"I know," said Chloe sadly. "I suppose it would be better than nothing." Privately, however, Chloe wondered if it would.

Back at the hotel they all grabbed a quick lunch before the dining room closed. Several girls came up to Chloe to say how sorry they were about her lost case, and Chloe texted Lolly to tell her about the failure to find a replacement dress for the concert.

The message had only just been sent when Chloe's mobile rang. It was Lolly!

"I've just texted you," said Chloe, enormously pleased to hear her best friend's voice.

"I got it. How's it going?" asked Lolly. "I'm so sorry we can't be with you at the moment. It sounds as if you could do with some support."

"Tara is doing her best," said Chloe, loyally. "And Mrs. Player is really nice, but they don't really understand. Or at least I think Tara does, but you know how she hates any sort of fuss about clothes."

Chloe could almost hear Lolly's brain whirring as she tried to think of another solution. "You see, Mrs. Sharkey won't let us send you anything," she explained. "She didn't want to risk getting any of our clothes lost as well. She said her insurance probably wouldn't cover it and our mum might be cross. I didn't tell her we'd lent you some of our things already! She was sure you'd find something in the shops. Hang on a minute."

Chloe waited while Lolly had a word with her sister. Chloe could hear them both talking and wished she was there with them. After a few moments Lolly came back on the phone.

"Pop thinks someone we modelled for in Milan a

couple of years ago has moved to the city you're in," she explained. "She's called Carlotta Bellini. She was going to start her own designer range, but we can't remember who it was she used to work for. If we could only remember, we could contact them and find out where Carlotta is. She was working on some lovely things when we saw her last."

"It's almost too late to go to any other shops," Chloe told her. "With rehearsals and things, and then the competition tomorrow night!"

"I know," said Lolly. "Look, leave it with us. We'll do our very best. Keep your fingers crossed."

"I will," agreed Chloe fervently. She said goodbye and switched off her mobile. She couldn't really see what else Pop and Lolly could do to help. They couldn't magic a fantastic dress out of thin air, but oh how she wished they could!

8 A Surprise for Chloe

Chloe had to put the lost dress out of her mind for the afternoon. Today was their chance to rehearse on the Battle of the Bands stage, and she needed to be totally focused for that. They didn't need to put much work into the actual song, because they had ironed out all the little problems back at Rockley Park. Ben had nailed the riff after lots of practice, and Tara had successfully altered the lyrics to help Chloe's breathing. But still, it was vital to feel comfortable onstage, and to make sure that their choreography would work in a space that they'd never performed in before.

While Danny was getting the drum kit arranged with his own snare, the others tuned up and plugged in their guitars. Chloe found her spot and walked through the movements she would make, humming the tune as she did so. It was important she didn't block the audience's view of the rest of the band, but she mustn't sing too far off to one side either. She had to make sure that they all looked as if they belonged together.

Mr. Player was standing down in the auditorium with Judge Jim, to see what they looked like onstage.

"How does it look?" asked Chloe, coming to the front of the stage.

"Good," said Judge Jim. "But what about usin' this part of the stage, where it juts out towards the audience?"

"I was wondering about that too," said Chloe, sitting down on the edge and dangling her legs over the side. "We didn't know the stage would be like this when we worked out my moves, but it would be good to use all the space if we can."

"Why not sing one verse down here?" suggested Mr. Player. "Then go back to the others for the last verse? It'll mean abandoning some of the movements you've worked on, but I think it would be worth it."

"I'd better discuss it with the others," said Chloe. "I don't want them thinking I'm trying to make it look as if they're just a backing band. This performance is about all of us together."

"Let's have a talk then," Judge Jim said. "You're right, Chloe. It has to be a joint decision."

"I'll go and get them," Chloe volunteered. She got to her feet and jogged over to the guitarists. Ed was having trouble with one of his strings going out of tune. He looked up as she reached him and grimaced.

"It's always like that when I put a new string on," he told her. "Don't worry. It'll be fine soon. It's just stretching a bit."

"We need to talk about the shape of the stage," Chloe said. "Judge Jim and Mr. Player want a word."

"Oh. Okay."

Soon, everyone was down at the front, sitting on the edge of the stage. Judge Jim explained the situation and Danny laughed. "Chloe can whizz about wherever she likes, as far as I'm concerned," he said. "I know you only want the best for the band, Chloe. I'm just grateful I don't have your job. I'd hate it!"

"As long as it looks as if she's still part of us," said Ben thoughtfully. "Over here it's a long way from the rest of us."

"I agree," said Ed.

Tara shrugged. "But nearer to the audience," she reminded them. "And surely that's a good thing."

"Why not move the whole band forward?" suggested Ed. "We could even put Danny's drums right down here at the front!"

"No thanks!" said Danny quickly. "I want to be at the back of the band as usual. Besides, Ben is used to looking at me towards the end of the song to check the timing of the last chord. He might forget where I was!"

"Okay. Okay!" said Tara. "But we could all come up to the front a *bit* more."

"Tara's right," agreed Judge Jim. "Just a couple of metres would make a big difference. Then Chloe could use this part of the stage an' you would still all be connected."

"I've just thought of something," said Ed. "One of my guitars has got a wireless pickup. Do you think that would work here? If so, would it help if I didn't need to be plugged in to play?"

"It would mean you could come right down here with Chloe," said Judge Jim, "without trailing a lead all over the place."

"Maybe Chloe could sing the middle verse to you," suggested Mr. Player. "The lyrics are very poignant, and it would be nice to have a focus for them."

"It would reinforce the band's connection too," said Ben. "Do you fancy being serenaded by Chloe, Ed?"

Ed looked a bit uncertain. "I don't know," he said. "But we could try it if you like."

There were plenty of technicians about, and it didn't take many minutes to move everyone forward. Unfortunately, the wireless connection was rather unreliable, and they had to abandon that idea.

"It's probably just as well," Ed smiled as they took their positions again. "You'd probably laugh, if you tried to sing and look at me!"

They ran through the song, and Chloe gave it everything she'd got. She was fine until the middle verse. *"I feel my life is through,"* she sang. *"I don't know what to do. Take away the grey today, and bring me back sky blue."*

For the first time, it hit her how apt the words were for the situation she was in. Her world *did* feel very grey at the moment, and she desperately wanted her sky-blue dress back. To her horror she felt tears of self-pity well up in her eyes, and in a second she was crying so hard she had to stop singing. For a few bars the others kept playing, but it was obvious that something was very wrong, and one by one they stopped.

"What's the matter?" asked Danny, getting up from his drum kit and going over to her.

"Sorry," sniffed Chloe, wiping her eyes. "I'll be all right in a minute."

She took some deep breaths and tried to smile, but it wasn't easy. Danny looked embarrassed and uncertain how to help her. "Is it nerves?" he asked.

Chloe shook her head vehemently. "No!" she told

him. "No. It's stupid. The lyrics made me think about my missing dress…and I just…" She could feel the tears coming again and tried furiously to push them away.

"But the song isn't anything to do with a dress," Danny told her, sounding rather bemused.

"I know that," said Chloe.

"Well…"

Now Mr. Player was coming onstage, and Chloe could see Judge Jim talking to another man down in the auditorium. Maybe he was from the next band scheduled to practise, and wanted them to hurry up. Chloe told herself to get a grip. If she didn't sort herself out quickly their rehearsal slot would be wasted.

"Chloe," said Mr. Player as soon as he reached her. "Anything I can help you with?"

"No, I'm sorry," said Chloe. "I'll be okay in a minute. Have we still got time for a run-through?"

"It's all right," he told her. "We've got loads of time. But I just thought you ought to know that Manny Williams is here."

"Manny Williams! What's he doing here?"

Manny Williams was a very famous independent producer, who liked to scout for new talent from time to time. He had expressed an interest in Chloe after she had performed so well at a Rising Stars concert, but they hadn't worked together yet. In fact, this was the first time she'd had the chance of seeing him.

Chloe looked down into the auditorium again. Manny Williams was talking to Judge Jim. He looked quite old, short-haired, and was very neatly dressed in a dark suit. He raised his hand to acknowledge Chloe and she waved back to him self-consciously.

"What does he want?" she asked Mr. Player.

Mr. Player shrugged. "I don't know. But he seemed to want you to know he was there. Don't worry. He's really nice, Chloe. He won't want you to freak out just because he's turned up." Mr. Player patted Chloe on the back and went back to join Judge Jim and Manny Williams again.

In spite of her teacher's reassurance, Chloe felt doubly pressured. It would be just her bad luck if Manny told her he'd changed his mind about working

with her now he'd seen her break down in the middle
of a song. After all, it was so unprofessional to cry like
that. She took another deep breath, and looked to
where Danny was, back behind his drums. "Shall we
try again?" she suggested.

"Okay."

Ben played the intro and the rest of the band came
in. Chloe lifted up the microphone and started to sing.
This time she kept her mind firmly away from anything
that might upset her voice, and when she got to the
middle verse she steadfastly refused to feel the words
at all. She enjoyed sashaying down to the projecting
part of the stage and dancing right out into the
auditorium. Then she ran back to the rest of the band
while they played the bridge and was with them to sing
the last verse and chorus.

They went through the finale of the song, their bows
and getting offstage. All that went without a hitch, and
so they joined the teachers in the auditorium, where
Mr. Player introduced them to Manny Williams. Chloe
wasn't exactly happy with her performance of the

middle verse, and she was worried about what Manny might think. She'd been so scared about breaking down again that she had given it no emotion at all, but she *was* pleased to have got through to the end.

"Well done," Judge Jim told the band. "Ben you were perfect this time. As were the rest of you," he added to the other musicians.

Chloe felt uncomfortable, and looked at her singing teacher. "What happened in the middle verse?" asked Mr. Player. "You usually sing it so well."

"Yes," added Manny Williams in a quiet voice. "If you sing like that tomorrow, there's no way you'll win the Battle of the Bands!"

9 A Helping Hand

Chloe looked at Manny Williams in horror. Was he, like Tara, someone who thought that straight talking was the only way to go? Couldn't he be a bit more gentle, and at least praise the bits she had sung well? Mr. Player was so good at boosting her ego, while at the same time helping her to improve.

As she stared at Manny he returned her gaze. He didn't smile, but his expression was friendly, and all at once she saw that she had to agree with what he had said. He was right; she couldn't deny it. There was no way they'd win if she sang with as little passion as that, but she hadn't been prepared to admit it to herself until he had put it into words.

Battle of the Bands

Manny's face held a lifetime of experience. And it reminded her that the music industry was a hard taskmaster. Manny had made lots of singers famous, but there was no room for error. You only got to the top by having something special, and you only kept your place if you worked hard at staying there. There was no point pretending. He would always tell it as it was, kindly, but honestly. She could totally trust him.

Chloe felt all this almost instantly. But Manny had already moved on.

"I'm here to scout for new talent," he told her. "But I'm glad to meet you today as well. I couldn't resist seeing how you are coping with such a big event." He paused, and looked at her sympathetically. "You are having emotional problems," he continued in a matter-of-fact voice. "We must attend to them, and see if we can make use of them. Tell me…"

He drew her away from the others, and Mr. Player nodded for her to follow the maestro. They sat a couple of rows away, and Chloe found herself telling Manny Williams what had so suddenly upset her. She could tell him easily. He was so calm, as if they were faced with a small technical problem that would soon be fixed.

Manny nodded sympathetically as Chloe spoke. Mr. Player must have given him a copy of the music and lyrics, because he had them in his hand. "There is a trigger here," Manny told her. "That set you off. The best art always speaks to us personally, and your friend has written a very accomplished song. What you have to do is use the emotion you feel without making it impossible to carry on singing."

Chloe nodded. "But how?" she asked.

"Some people manage it by standing outside themselves. They recognize the emotion, and feel it greatly, but keep a core of calmness that doesn't allow the emotion to get out of hand."

"It sounds very difficult," said Chloe doubtfully.

"It can be," Manny agreed. "Some people never manage it, but it's worth a try. By singing the words *sky blue* and *grey*, you were reminded about your missing dress and how worried you are about it. If you can make the anxiety less specific and feel a more general sadness inside yourself, you may find that instead of hiccups and a runny nose, you can produce just one, perfect tear, which will wow the audience."

Chloe couldn't help laughing, and Manny laughed with her. "If it helps, think of your emotions simply as brain chemicals," he told her. "You *can* be in charge. Let just the right amount out and you will get that perfect tear, too much and you'll be a total mess."

"It sounds scary," said Chloe.

"It is," agreed Manny. "But life is all about taking risks. Try it."

"Now?"

"Yes. Think of the music and sing the words, softly, but with the same intensity as you do onstage. There's a tipping point. If you can almost reach that point and hold it there you'll be in control."

Chloe did as he suggested. She imagined herself onstage, giving the song everything she'd got. She had always loved the words, but Manny was right, they did fill her with sadness. She sang quietly, letting her feelings run free, but when she got to the middle verse she lost her nerve. She sang it well, very well, but she knew that she could have risked just a bit more.

When she glanced at Manny she could see that he knew exactly what she'd done. He smiled slightly. "Keep trying," he told her. "Your band is completely together. It's musically one of the tightest young bands I've seen, so there are no worries there. Your voice is staggeringly beautiful and pitch perfect. You have the right look too. Believe me, that's important, even at your age. But there are lots of excellent bands and singers here. The competition is fierce, and under those circumstances you need something very special. If you can go out there and appear on those big screens with a few tears at the right moment, you will disarm the audience and the judges, because the expression in your voice and the tears in your eyes will prove how much you feel the music."

Manny Williams got up. "And now I must go," he told Chloe. He shook her hand formally and bowed slightly from the waist. "I will be in the audience tomorrow, and will be watching with great interest."

Without another word he set off down the long aisle towards the exit. He was very different from everyone else Chloe had met in the music industry. She watched him go with mixed feelings. Chloe felt disappointed that he hadn't wished her good luck, but then she realized he probably wasn't the sort of person to believe in luck. He believed in hard work, determination and courage. And he had told her that her voice was beautiful. She wouldn't share that with anyone, they might think she was bragging, but she would treasure his words for ever.

"Are you okay?" asked Tara, when Chloe rejoined the rest of the band.

Chloe nodded. "He is the most amazing person I've ever met," she told them in an awed voice.

"He has got fantastic insight, hasn't he?" agreed Mr. Player. "If he ever wanted to come and teach at Rockley Park I'd be out of a job!"

"I'm not sure how good he'd be at teaching a class," Chloe told Mr. Player loyally.

"I think your job is safe," agreed Judge Jim. "Chloe's right. He's a bit of an oddball. Strictly a one-to-one sort of person."

"So did he give you a few tips?" asked Ed.

"Mmm," said Chloe. "He did, and I'm going to do the very best I can to do what he suggested."

"What *did* he suggest?" asked Ben.

Chloe frowned. "It's difficult to explain," she said, wanting to keep Manny's advice to herself.

"Well, does he think we're in with a chance?" asked Danny anxiously.

"Yes," said Chloe firmly. "He does, and he said that we were one of the most together young bands he'd seen."

Danny smiled one of his wide smiles. "That's great!" he said.

It was almost time to go back. The hotel was laying on entertainment for the students after dinner, and Chloe's stomach was telling her that it would soon time to eat. But before they left the venue they spent a few minutes watching the next band come onstage to practise. They were a heavy metal band and even though they didn't play Chloe's kind of music, they were great fun to watch.

"Let's get back. I want a shower, and something to eat and drink," urged Ben.

"Me too," agreed Tara. "I'm starving."

"Okay," said Judge Jim. "We've done well with your rehearsal slot. You've had a run-through, sorted out how to use the space onstage an' Chloe has had a surprise visit from maestro Manny. That must be enough for one afternoon!"

It wasn't long before they were back at the hotel. Chloe and Tara were just getting into the lift when one of the receptionists called to Chloe.

"There is someone to see you," she said. "She has been waiting for a while."

"Where?" asked Tara.

"Who is it?" added Chloe.

The woman pointed to a group of comfortable chairs set to one side of the reception area. There was only one person there. Chloe looked at the person and then at Tara.

"Do you know her?" asked Tara.

"No," said Chloe in a very puzzled voice. "I've never seen her before in my life!"

10 A Welcome Visitor

The person waiting was a young woman. She got up as Chloe and Tara approached and looked from one girl to the other.

"I'm Chloe," said Chloe helpfully.

"Ah." She offered her hand and Chloe shook it. "I am Carlotta Bellini," she said, offering Chloe a card. Chloe racked her brains. She knew she'd heard the name recently, but couldn't remember where. A glance at Tara's face made it obvious that Tara was none the wiser.

"I brought some things," said Carlotta, pointing to two large boxes.

"Have you?" said Chloe, wondering what was in

them. Then in a rush she remembered. Carlotta Bellini was the name of the designer Lolly had mentioned!

"Oh!" she exclaimed so suddenly that Tara jumped. "Lolly told me about you. But how...?"

Carlotta grinned. "Pop and Lolly, they are very persuasive," she told Chloe. "First Lolly telephones and tells me of your problem. Then Pop telephones and says I must go *at once,* and so I bring everything I can in their size because they say you are the same and I think now, yes, it is almost true."

"That's *amazing,*" said Chloe. "Thank you *so* much. I'm sorry you've been waiting so long."

"No problem," said Carlotta. "But if you like we can go and try?"

"Of course!" agreed Chloe.

"I'll help carrying," offered Tara.

They went up in the lift together and into Tara and Chloe's room. Carlotta took the lid off the first box and pulled aside some layers of tissue. As she lifted the first dress out Chloe gasped. "It's beautiful!"

It *was* a beautiful dress. It was midnight blue satin,

and the skirt swished and swung as Carlotta held it up.

"I'll go and tell Mrs. Player!" said Tara. She raced out of the door, but Chloe didn't even notice her go. She was staring, with eyes like saucers, as Carlotta drew dress after dress out of the boxes. By the time Tara came back with Mrs. Player, seven wonderful dresses were hanging up in the open wardrobe.

"Oh, Chloe. What fantastic colours!" said Mrs. Player.

Chloe introduced her to Carlotta and the two women shook hands. "You are very kind to come," said Mrs. Player.

"It is no problem," said Carlotta graciously. "I hope Chloe can find what she needs. I am working on a new collection at the moment," she went on. "But these are from an exhibition I took part in two years ago. I wasn't long out of design college then, and I wanted people to get to know my name. These dresses are part of my 'Rainbow' collection that Pop and Lolly modelled for me. I trade under the name of Rainbow Designs now."

"Can I try this one on?" asked Chloe, pointing at a dress in a paler shade of blue.

"Of course," said Carlotta with a lovely smile. "In fact, this is the one Lolly said you would probably choose, as it is a similar colour to the one that has been lost."

Chloe put it on. She needed some help, because it was a very slim-fitting dress. When it was on, she went to the mirror in the bathroom to see what it looked like. It was a stunning design, with lines of stitching running up the front, accentuating the shape. It had long sleeves, and they were tight too, with the front of the sleeve coming to a point midway down Chloe's hand.

Chloe took several deep breaths, to see how it would feel to sing in it. When she came back out she was looking pensive.

"It is a little long, but that is no problem," said Carlotta.

"What do you think?" asked Mrs. Player.

Chloe wanted to say that it was perfect. But that wasn't true. The top was much too tight. The colour was lovely, and the cut was to die for, but she had to be honest: if she sang in this dress it would restrict her breathing, which was bad news for a singer. Chloe was worried the dress might rip at the seams if she took too big a breath, and that wouldn't be good at all.

Chloe didn't know how she was going to admit any of this, but Carlotta noticed that the sleeves were tight as soon as Chloe turned around.

"I am sorry. This one is no good for you," she said, touching Chloe's shoulder. "The fabric is being pulled out of shape here. I could alter this part but I think it would still pull there. The only thing to do would be to take the sleeves out altogether and that would unbalance the design."

"I think so too," Chloe agreed gratefully.

"How about the green one?" suggested Mrs. Player.

"Would it go with the band's clothes?" asked Tara.

"Try it on anyway," urged Carlotta.

The green dress was a design triumph. The fabric glistened like water, and it had a fishtail train at the back. Lines of beading swung like loops of pearls as Chloe moved. Chloe wished she could take it home with her, but it wasn't the right colour for the Battle of the Bands song and everyone agreed on that.

"The dark one?"

"Yes please."

"Wow!" Even Tara liked the midnight blue satin. It fitted Chloe almost perfectly, although Carlotta insisted that it would have to be altered slightly at the waist. It didn't restrict Chloe's breathing, and although it wasn't *sky* blue it was a beautiful colour. Chloe walked up and down in it. It was almost perfect, and she liked it. She liked it very much, but a tiny part of her was disappointed. For some reason the design seemed rather old fashioned. The sleeves were trumpet-like, and they reminded her of medieval paintings. Wizard Monkey Breath Scares the Horses was a rock band, not a band of minstrels.

"It's perfect," breathed Mrs. Player. She sounded so pleased. The past couple of days had been a nightmare and it was obvious how relieved she was that the panic was over. Chloe had her dress, and everyone could relax. Thank goodness.

"All you have to do is get some shoes tomorrow and you're fixed," said Tara, gazing at the dress Chloe was wearing with satisfaction. "And we know where to go for those."

Tara was obviously doing her best to join in with the clothes talk, and she was doing quite well, but Chloe could see that she was at least as relieved as Mrs. Player.

Chloe took a deep breath. Well, as far as she was concerned, the dress wasn't perfect, but it fitted, the colour was fine, and she had it in time for the competition. Things could have been so much worse. She could live with this one, and if it didn't look quite right, well, no one could say they hadn't all done their best.

She turned to Carlotta to thank her, but the designer was looking puzzled.

"Something is missing," she said. "I was sure I had…" She went over to a box and pulled all the white tissue out into a heap on the floor. She scratched her head and went to the other box. "Ah!" She threw another heap of rustling tissue aside and looked at Chloe. "I'm sorry," she said. "I had packed eight dresses, but I forgot this one when I was unpacking the others. It was hidden by the tissue, and only now I remember to look. Don't decide until you try."

Out of the box she drew a pure white dress. It was simple, but quite beautiful. Soft white feathers cascaded from the left shoulder, across and down the length of the dress. They did the same at the back, and at the bottom of the dress, almost at the hem, was an embroidered rainbow.

Chloe scrambled out of the blue dress and into the white one. It was perfect. On every feather sparkled a small crystal, each one like the perfect tear Manny had talked about that afternoon. Chloe knew it was the right dress even before she put it on, and once she was wearing it, there could be no argument.

"This one," she said to Carlotta, her face a picture of pure joy. "*This* is the one!"

11 Competition Day

The next day dawned as clear and sunny as the last few had been. Chloe woke early, and for a few minutes she lay still, thinking about the white dress. She was the happiest she'd been since she'd arrived in Italy. At last, everything was going right, and just in time. The Battle of the Bands was tonight! A bubble of excitement welled up inside her; she couldn't stay put a minute longer, so she stole out of bed and opened the door to the balcony as quietly as possible, so as not to wake Tara.

Chloe could see the early morning sun creeping along the hotel wall towards her, but for now the balcony was in shade, so the floor tiles were cool under her bare feet. She decided to practise her song, with Manny's advice in mind, so she pulled the door to behind her and went through her usual warming-up exercises. Then, facing out over the city, and looking towards the distant blue hills, Chloe began to sing. The words floated out into the air, and she knew she was singing the best she ever had. In her mind's eye the others were there too, playing as they had never played before. They had the audience in the palm of their hands. Together they were unstoppable.

As she reached the middle verse Chloe searched for the right amount of melancholy to give the words the pathos they needed, without letting herself tip over into uncontrollable tears.

She sang it really well, and a few days earlier would have been totally satisfied, but since her talk with Manny she knew she could still do better. However, this morning she felt so happy it was impossible to conjure up enough sadness. It was so good to feel this way, that she didn't mind about anything else. She was just grateful to be able to smile again. As she finished the song she was very pleased. Her voice was on top form, and she felt ready for anything. Then a sound behind her made her turn round. It was Tara, clapping.

"Well done," said Tara. "That was brilliant. You made it sound so good I almost forgot that I wrote it!"

"It's a great song," Chloe told her. "And I feel so good that I'm sure we'll do well with it tonight."

"I'll be happy as long as we do better than those awful, squealing Pink Toffee girls," said Tara. "If they win their category I'll…well I don't know what I'll do."

"That's not very patriotic," giggled Chloe.

"Maybe not, but they don't make me feel very patriotic," grumbled Tara. "They are just so *silly*."

"At least the rest of our country's bands are okay," said Chloe. "I like both the senior bands, don't you?"

"Yes I do," Tara agreed. "And I suppose three out of four isn't so bad."

"I'm going to have my shower now," said Chloe, going over to the box of goodies Cat and Suzy had brought her. "It's so lovely to have these things, but I don't know which to choose!"

"Well just hurry up and decide," said Tara. "It must almost be breakfast time, and I'm starving."

Straight after breakfast everyone made their way to the coaches waiting to take all the competitors to the venue. It was still early morning, but they wanted to be there as soon as possible to soak up the atmosphere and get their soundchecks done. Carlotta had taken the white dress to alter the hem slightly and would bring it to the venue later, so Chloe was free to enjoy the day.

The venue was thronging with people. Students were streaming in from all directions. Some were busy, but others were sitting around, chatting and watching the latest soundcheck taking place. Chloe's heart started beating faster. This was what she liked better than anything, to be caught up in the business of getting a gig ready.

There was no time to stand and stare though, as it was almost time for their own soundcheck. The band members left the teachers and went backstage to wait for their name to be called. As soon as it was they hurried onstage, passing the last band coming off.

Competition Day

Chloe stood at her microphone and waited while Danny checked that his snare drum was ready for him. Then the engineer asked him to begin. Some musicians play a lot louder than others, and he needed to know what sort of drummer Danny was. Drums are the most complex instruments in a band, so it is usual to begin the soundcheck by sorting them out. There was a microphone on each drum and cymbal, and each one had to be tested individually for sound. The engineer had to make a note of the levels needed by every drummer for each microphone so it was a painstaking business. But it was vitally important to feed just the right amount of sound from each microphone into the speakers, so the audience wasn't straining to hear one moment and being blasted out of their seats at the next. Once the correct level had been set for all the drum microphones, the guitar and voice mics could be set to match them.

Ben followed Danny. He played a few bars for the engineer, then Ed and Tara did the same. At last, the engineer asked Chloe to sing something into her microphone and she tried out the chorus of their song.

"Okay," said the engineer. "*Tutti insieme.*"

He waved his arms in wide circles, to explain what he meant, so they didn't need a translation. They could all see that he wanted the whole band to play together now. That was good. It meant there weren't any problems; he just wanted to check the sound level when everything was put together.

Chloe looked out into the auditorium. Later on the seating would be in darkness, but for now the main lights were up and she could see everybody there. Some students down near the front were watching intently, and she realized it was The Wildcats when she noticed Cat. Chloe wondered if Danny had seen them.

They all played in perfect time, and Chloe gave the song everything she'd got. As soon as they'd finished, the engineer gave a thumbs up. "Okay. You are finish. *Grazie.*"

Chloe and the boys grinned at each other. The check had gone well, and the run-through had been great. Danny undid his snare and handed it to the technician, while Chloe put her microphone back on its stand.

"Okay!" said Ben, giving Chloe a slap on her back as they headed offstage. "It was mega, wasn't it, Chloe? We've given those other bands something to think about!"

"I wonder if The Wildcats have done their soundcheck yet?" said Chloe. "I'd like to hear them."

"Cat told me they were doing theirs shortly after us," Danny said, joining the others at the side of the stage. The next band was up. The boy vocalists had already handed their backing track to the engineer and were waiting for their instructions. "Let's go to the front and watch this lot. Maybe The Wildcats will be on after them."

Sure enough, when they got to the front they could only say a quick hello before Cat and her fellow band members had to get in place for their check.

"Fantastic song!" said Cat, kissing both Chloe and Danny on both cheeks. "Danny, you are great drummer. I'm glad we have competition with Pink Toffee, not you! I think it will be hard for any band to beat you."

Danny looked very pleased. "Good luck with your soundcheck," he told her.

"See you afterwards," said Chloe. But then an announcement in English came over the sound system.

"*Chloe Tompkins to backstage reception. Chloe Tompkins to backstage reception.*"

"I wonder what they want me for?" she wondered. "It must be Carlotta with my dress. She had to take the hem up a little bit."

"Well you'd better go and see," said Ben.

"What a shame. You'll miss The Wildcats' soundcheck," said Danny.

"You'll have to tell me all about it," said Chloe regretfully.

She hurried through the pass door and into the backstage area. There was a small booth nearby, which she assumed must be the reception. When she gave her name she was told to go to the costume room. *Brilliant,* she thought to herself. *Carlotta is here with the dress. It's going to be fantastic wearing it onstage. I know I'll be able to sing at my best tonight, thanks to her. I can't wait!*

12 Just in Time

Chloe rushed eagerly into the costume room. Mrs. Player was there, and so was Carlotta – with the glorious dress swathed in plastic, and draped over her arm. But there were two other people waiting for her as well. Chloe couldn't believe her eyes.

"LOLLY! POP! What are you doing here?" asked Chloe in amazement.

"Isn't it fantastic?" squealed Pop, giving Chloe a huge hug.

"Mrs. Sharkey gave us permission to come, after all the hard work we'd put in finding you another dress," explained Lolly, hugging Chloe as well. "And Mum said she'd bring us because she wanted to come shopping here anyway. She loves the shops in this city."

"I'm *so* glad you're here," said Chloe. "And Tara will be too. She's had a terrible time pretending to like clothes for my sake."

"You're going to look amazing in this dress," said Lolly. "Carlotta has been showing us. We knew she'd come up trumps."

"Yes," agreed Pop. "Her designs are just perfect." She gave the designer a big hug too, and Carlotta laughed.

"I am glad to help," she said. "And it will be good for me – to dress Chloe at this big event. Thank you for giving me the opportunity. Now let's make sure I altered the hem so it is perfect."

As soon as the wardrobe mistress saw Chloe in Carlotta's dress, she threw up her hands in admiration. She was covered in smiles, as Carlotta spoke to her rapidly in Italian. Chloe turned round several times so Carlotta could check that her alterations were right.

"*Perfetto*," Carlotta proclaimed at last, and the wardrobe mistress agreed. "Now, where can we put this so that nothing terrible happens to it?" asked the designer.

The wardrobe mistress set off in a torrent of Italian again and whisked the dress away.

"Don't worry," said Carlotta with a grin. "She says she will guard it with her life!"

Mrs. Player was looking at her watch. "We should go and have something to eat," she told Chloe. "If you have a good lunch now you won't need to eat again before the competition starts later on this afternoon. You don't want to sing on a full stomach, do you?"

"You're right," Chloe agreed. "Are we all going together?"

"Of course!" her friends answered.

"We're hungry too," explained Lolly. "And it's going to be a long night."

It didn't take long to find the boys. Carlotta joined them in the canteen as well and soon they were all eating pasta together. It was almost like being back at school, but Carlotta's company made things a bit different. When Cat and her band arrived for their lunch, Chloe suggested they all sit together. Things got quite noisy, but no one seemed to mind. Danny and Cat spent almost as much time gazing at each other as eating. Chloe exchanged glances with Tara and they both grinned. "I didn't get a chance to hear The Wildcats sing," Chloe said. "Were they good?"

Tara nodded. "They were brilliant. Four girls and a boy are a bit different, and they were quirky too." Chloe followed her gaze to The Wildcats' boy singer, who had very long, dark hair. He looked up and smiled at Tara, who, to Chloe's great surprise, blushed and dipped her head. *Wow!* thought Chloe. *I've never seen Tara behave like that before.*

Soon it was time to go and get changed. Chloe, Tara and the boys exchanged hugs with Pop, Lolly and Carlotta. They wouldn't be seeing them again until after the competition was over.

"Good luck," they all told each other. "Good luck!"

Chloe wanted to be totally focused by the time she had to go onstage and sing the song. She knew the boys and Tara would be trying to clear their minds of any clutter too. From now until after it was all over, they simply had to concentrate on being the best band ever.

Mrs. Player stayed to help Chloe, but soon after she was ready, all non-performers were asked to leave the backstage area. Chloe and Tara went to the green room, where the boys were already waiting. She felt wonderful in her white dress and stage make-up, which Mrs. Player had done beautifully for her, in spite of Chloe's worries about her not being very stylish.

"Wow!" said Danny admiringly, when he saw Chloe in her new dress. "You look great!"

Chloe was pleased at the compliment, but everyone was feeling the tension now, even her. Apart from some venue employees there were only students in the green room, all waiting nervously for the International Battle of the Bands to commence.

There were speakers and a TV screen so that the students would be able to watch the other bands performing. There was a roving cameraman too. His shots were being relayed to the enormous screen in the auditorium, where the audience was filling the seats. As soon as the competition began it would be beamed out live on TV. Thousands of people would be watching the show.

And somewhere in the audience were Judge Jim, Mr. and Mrs. Player, Manny Williams and Carlotta, along with Pop and Lolly. Chloe knew they would be cheering for Wizard Monkey Breath Scares the Horses, but she was certain she wouldn't be able to hear them. They were so few amongst the vast audience. But still, she knew they were there, and that was enough. Plus there was her old friend Jess from Chloe's last school. Chloe was sure Jess would be watching back in England with her mates.

Then, with a pang, Chloe thought of her family at home. It would have been wonderful if they could have been here tonight, but that was impossible. Instead, Chloe could picture her mum and dad sitting on the sofa together, with her little brother between them. He would be very excited to be allowed to stay up late to see his big sister on the TV. Chloe wondered if he'd recognize her in her make-up and feather dress. Home seemed a world away from Chloe's life now.

For a while, Cat and Danny sat together, but as the time wore on they gave each other a hug and moved to be with their respective bands. Everyone needed to focus now.

A huge cheer went up as the concert presenters arrived onstage. Chloe almost wished she were in the audience. It looked and sounded fantastic on the screen in the green room as the performances began. But she would be onstage soon herself, and that would be better still.

Now Cat and her band were standing up, and threading their way between groups of students to reach the door. The other Italian bands waved flags and cheered.

Chloe and the boys watched The Wildcats closely. Chloe was particularly interested, as she hadn't seen them perform before. As they brought their song to a terrific conclusion Chloe felt a bit sorry for Pink Toffee. Their performance had been nothing like as good as

Battle of the Bands

The Wildcats'. Chloe didn't like Pink Toffee's style very much, but it would be horrible to be so outclassed.

The Wildcats came off to tumultuous applause. After all, not only were they brilliant, but they also had the home crowd behind them. It would be very difficult for *any* band in that category to beat such a bravura performance.

"I think we were pretty good? No?" said Cat as she arrived back in the green room, fired up with excitement. In her enthusiasm she kissed everyone within reach.

Soon there were only three bands to go before the whole competition would be over. Most of the students who had already performed were relaxed, but the tension was still very high for Chloe, Tara and the boys. They had known they would be one of the last bands to perform, but waiting wasn't easy. Now, at last, they made their way to the backstage area, where an official was waiting to send them on at exactly the right time. They stood together, listening to the band onstage. Ben, Ed and Tara had their instruments slung over their shoulders, and Danny was clutching several pairs of drumsticks. Chloe concentrated on taking slow, even breaths. Her heart was thumping against her ribs and she felt almost sick with nerves and excitement.

Then, just when she didn't want any distractions, Chloe started to think about her mum and dad. How she wished they could have been here to see her perform. But she knew it was impossible. She would just have to cope without them, and it was too late to ask any of the band members for a comforting word now.

Chloe looked down at her dress. The feathers were moving softly in the air and the crystals sparkled and gave her courage. Yes, she did miss her family very much, but she also felt in control.

And then the official took hold of Chloe's arm. He waited until he got a signal in his earpiece. "*Adesso!*" he said urgently and thrust Chloe towards the stage. "*Vai.*"

Chloe walked briskly onto the stage with her head up, her shoulders back, and a smile on her face. The others ran on and plugged in as quickly as they could. Danny slid behind the drum kit. Chloe reached her microphone. Everyone was ready. The feathers on Chloe's beautiful white dress trembled under the hot lights, and the crystals glittered like diamonds. It was time to sing.

13 A Song and Another Surprise

Suddenly, a rainbow of lights showered colour over Chloe, and the white dress lit up in a thousand flashes of brilliance. It could have been made especially for this very moment! Ben played the opening bars of "Sky Blue", and Chloe counted herself in, paying close attention to Danny's beat. Up there under the lights, part of Chloe felt breathless with excitement, but another part of her, the professional singer in her, was cool and collected. She had a job to do, and she was going to do it to the very best of her ability.

Once she started singing she was in complete control. She remembered her steps perfectly. Even when the mirrored floor beneath her feet lit up and threw more flashes of light at her, she didn't flinch. She sang the first verse perfectly, and moved downstage to sing the middle one.

And she hadn't forgotten her conversation with Manny. Could she bring that bit extra to her performance? It was a huge risk. If she made a mess of it she would be letting down the band, the school and her country. But didn't she equally owe it to them to try her very best? Hadn't Manny thought they needed something extra if they were going to have a chance of winning?

As the boys played the bridge between one verse and the next, Chloe wavered. She wasn't given to self-pity as a rule, but as the middle verse approached she felt the sadness of her family not being with her on this biggest challenge of her life. Her mum and dad *should* have been here to cheer her on. She felt like crying.

"*I feel my life is through,*" she sang. "*I don't know what to do.*"

But Chloe wasn't going to let her emotions control her. She *did* know what to do, and she was still in charge, however sad she felt. There was a tipping point, and she had reached it. She mustn't, simply *mustn't* go over the edge.

Her voice was full of heartbreaking sadness, and as the music swelled to the climax of the verse she turned to the audience, hidden in the darkness of the auditorium. Thousands of people all around the world were watching and listening at home too, but Chloe sang as if to each person alone.

"Take away the grey today," she begged.

There was a little break in her voice as she faltered. The audience held its breath as tears welled up in Chloe's eyes. It was as if they were intruding on some private grief. Two perfect tears trickled slowly down her cheeks as she waited for the right moment to sing the last line.

"And bring me back sky blue."

It had been totally quiet in the auditorium, but now a sigh went up as the audience felt the emotion with her.

Somehow, Chloe got herself back to the band and

calmed herself, ready for the final verse. She didn't dare wipe her tears away, in case she smudged her stage make-up, so she left them where they were, glistening on her cheeks.

The last verse was much more upbeat, and she handled it deftly, totally at one with the band. The climax was a few bars away, then a few notes and then they all finished as one, with perfect timing. Chloe put her microphone gently back on its stand and the audience erupted into cheers and shouts. She looked back at the rest of the band and grinned. The noise was far too loud for her to hear what any of them were saying, but they all looked pretty pleased.

Every band had been given strict instructions not to milk their applause, but to get off as soon as possible after they'd finished. Wizard Monkey Breath Scares the Horses gave a quick bow and ran offstage, waving to the audience as they went. Even so, thunderous applause followed them, and was still going on as they made their way back to the green room.

"I think they liked it," said Danny. "Well done us."

A Song and Another Surprise

"We gave it our best shot," said Ben. "I don't know what else we could have done."

"They more than liked it," said Tara with a wide grin on her face. "Listen to that!"

The presenters were having trouble calming the audience down so they could move on to the last band. Then the voting could begin.

Back in the green room lots of bands gave Wizard Monkey Breath a cheer. Cat came straight up to Danny and kissed his cheek. Then she hugged all the other members of the band. Last of all, she went up to Chloe.

"Are you all right?" she asked anxiously. "You were so sad onstage. I am sorry if something is wrong."

"No. Nothing is wrong," Chloe assured her. "It's fine. In fact, now it's over I feel fantastic. It's over!"

It was true. After all the stress and anxiety of the missing dress, the hard work making the song the best it could be, and the nervousness before going on, they could all finally relax. They couldn't influence the voting now, whatever they did, so they might as well enjoy the party. And it *was* turning into a party in the green room.

Battle of the Bands

Now all the performances were done the tension was gone for the time being and everyone could relax. Even with the results still to come, everyone looked happy.

The judges deliberated during the break, and lots of text messages came flying onto the student's mobiles from their friends and relations. Absolutely everyone was checking their mobiles and comparing messages. Then one came in for Chloe. It was from her old school friend, Jess. *How cool am I, knowing you!* it said. That made Chloe laugh.

But there was a message missing, one Chloe wanted very much. Even Tara's busy parents had managed to send her a text, but Chloe was still waiting. She waited so long she was beginning to think they'd never send one, but just as she was about to give up hope, it came in.

It was a picture message. Her little brother was grinning and holding up a notice that said, *Hurray for Chloe!* There was a text too. *What a wonderful daughter we've got,* it said. *We're so proud of you. What a star you are. Love M & D xxx*

A Song and Another Surprise

Now Chloe had a big lump in her throat, and for a while she couldn't speak. Part of her wanted nothing more than to be with her family at home this very minute, but then she looked around the crowded green room. She saw Danny, Tara and the others all chattering excitedly, and suddenly the homesickness was gone. There would be plenty of time for hugs with her family when Chloe got back.

But now it was almost time for the results to be announced, and everyone in the green room was getting twitchy. Only a few could be winners tonight, and many students would go home disappointed, but it had been a fantastic occasion and everyone would leave with some happy memories.

When it was time for the junior vocalists class to be announced, Cat and her band members stood clutching each other's hands in silence, while the Pink Toffee girls gabbled wildly in anticipation. Chloe couldn't help hoping that The Wildcats would win their section.

"And next," said the presenter onstage, "we come to the winner of the junior vocalists."

Battle of the Bands

The whole room fell silent, as everyone stared at the TV screen. Everything was announced in Italian first, and then English, so it was important to listen carefully. As soon as the presenter said the words Pink Toffee the girls from the band began screaming in delight. They obviously thought they had won, but the presenter was still speaking, and it was clear to Chloe that the winner hadn't actually been announced yet. After a couple more sentences the crowd broke into enthusiastic cheers and The Wildcats leaped up and down looking ecstatic.

Slowly, the Pink Toffee girls realized that they had been mistaken. Several of them burst into tears.

"Don't waste your sympathy," Tara growled at Chloe. "They didn't deserve to beat The Wildcats." This was undeniably true, but they had contributed to Chloe's box of goodies and she couldn't help feeling sorry for them, so she went over to commiserate.

"And now..." said the announcer. Everyone fell silent as Chloe made her way back to her band. This was their category at last. "The junior band..."

A Song and Another Surprise

Everyone in Wizard Monkey Breath Scares the Horses held their breath. The preamble seemed to go on for ages, and several bands were named, including Chloe's. But none of the band members were counting on anything. They were all waiting for the translation to tell them which one had actually won, but before it came Cat started hugging Danny, a grin all over her face.

"*Vittoria!*" she yelled. "You win! We both win! Now we must both perform again!"

Chloe returned hugs from the band while still listening.

"And the winner is…Wizard Monkey Breath…"

No one waited for the whole name to be announced. Chloe and the others were already jumping up and down with joy.

When it was their turn to go out and sing again it was impossible for Chloe to bring any sort of sadness to the song. She and the rest of the band were grinning throughout, but nobody minded. It became a storming rock-and-roll finale, with everyone clapping in time to the music. And when the applause died down, there was still a reception to go to, and photographers to smile for.

At the reception, Manny Williams found Chloe and took her hands in his. "You have real star quality," he told her.

Chloe blushed. "Thanks," she said. "And thanks for the advice you gave me too. I could never have done it without your help."

"It is one thing to have talent," replied Manny seriously, "but you also listen to advice and can act on it. Your voice and performance were outstanding tonight, young Chloe. I *so* look forward to working with you very soon."

It was very late indeed by the time they got back to the hotel, but even the hotel staff were ready to make a fuss of them. Eventually, the girls managed to make their way to the lift. Pop and Lolly had begged their mum to let them stay with Chloe, so the hotel staff had found camp beds for them. It would be a squeeze, but all four girls would be sleeping in the same room, just like at school.

A Song and Another Surprise

It was a hot night, and they went out onto the balcony for a breath of air.

"Isn't it nice to be quiet at last?" said Chloe.

"It has been an *amazing* night," said Lolly.

"And it's not over yet," said Tara, gazing out towards the dark hills. "Is that fireworks? Or is it lightning?"

As she spoke, a rumble of thunder echoed around the city and a brilliant flash of lightning lit up the sky.

"My turn to be entertained," said Chloe, sitting down and leaning her elbows on the balcony table. "I love storms."

So they all sat and watched, as the sky lit up like stage lights and the thunder crashed like a drum. Then Chloe had a sudden thought, and turned to Pop and Lolly with a worried expression.

"What's the matter?" asked Lolly.

"There's only one sad thing," Chloe told her. "My missing suitcase. I borrowed all those things from you and can't give them back."

"Don't worry about it," said Lolly. "Anyway, the case might still turn up after we fly home. Maybe it never even made it to Italy."

"Besides," giggled Pop. "Mum's always telling us we have far too many clothes in our wardrobe. Maybe you did us a favour!"

"You're such good friends," sighed Chloe. "I am lucky."

"So are you happy now?" asked Lolly.

"Oh yes," said Chloe. "What a wonderful time I've had. When I started at Rockley Park I didn't even consider singing in a band. I thought I was going to be this mega solo star, onstage all on my own."

"You still might," said Pop. "You have an awesome voice."

"Maybe," said Chloe, remembering what Manny had said about her voice, as a series of lightning flashes lit up the sky like celebratory fireworks. "But that doesn't matter, does it? All I do know is that it has been the most fantastic thing in the world to have won the Battle of the Bands." She beamed at them all.

"Especially with the help of my friends!"

✹ So you want
to be a pop star?

✹

Turn the page to read some top tips
on how to make your dreams
✹ come true... ✹

✳ Making it in the music biz ✳

Think you've got tons of talent?
Well, music maestro Judge Jim Henson,
Head of Rock at top talent academy Rockley
Park, has put together his hot tips to help
you become a superstar...

✳ Number One Rule: Be positive!
You've got to believe in yourself.

✳ Be active! Join your school choir
or form your own band.

✳ Be different! Don't be afraid to stand
out from the crowd.

✳ Be determined! Work hard and stay focused.

✳ Be creative! Try writing your own material –
it will say something unique about you.

✳ Be patient! Don't give up if things
don't happen overnight.

 Be ready to seize opportunities
when they come along.

Be versatile! Don't have a one-track mind – try out new things and gain as many skills as you can.

Be passionate! Don't be afraid to show some emotion in your performance.

Be sure to watch, listen and learn all the time.

Be willing to help others. You'll learn more that way.

Be smart! Don't neglect your school work.

Be cool and don't get big-headed! Everyone needs friends, so don't leave them behind.

 Always stay true to yourself.

And finally, and most importantly, enjoy what you do!

Go for it! It's all up to you now...

Usborne Quicklinks

For links to exciting websites where you can find out more about becoming a pop star and even practise your singing with online karaoke, go to the Usborne Quicklinks Website at www.usborne-quicklinks.com and enter the keywords "fame school".

Internet safety

When using the Internet make sure you follow these safety guidelines:

 Ask an adult's permission before using the Internet.

 Never give out personal information, such as your name, address or telephone number.

If a website asks you to type in your name or e-mail address, check with an adult first.

If you receive an e-mail from someone you don't know, do not reply to it.